Sleeping Beauty

Retold by Kate Knighton

Illustrated by
Jana Costa

Reading Consultant: Alison Kelly
Roehampton University

Contents

Chapter 1

Good news

Many years ago, a king and queen lived in a magical castle. They had everything they could want except...

...a baby. Year after year, the
queen stitched
and sewed
tiny clothes.

And the king made toys in
his palace workshop. But still
there was no baby.

Then, one day, while the queen sat knitting by the lake, a bright green frog

hopped...

skipped...

and jumped...

right onto her lap.

"Don't be sad, Your Majesty," said the frog. "You are going to have a baby this year."

And, with that, he bowed and leaped back into the lake.

True to the frog's words, the queen gave birth — to a lovely baby girl.

"I shall call her Rose," she declared happily.

The king was so pleased
he planned a feast to
celebrate.

"I shall invite every prince
and princess in the land!" he
decided, and asked seven fairies
to be Rose's fairy godmothers.

8

The king sent the invitations
by bluebird post – and
everyone agreed to come.

Servants scrubbed and
cleaned until the castle
gleamed. There had never
been a party like it.

Chapter 2

Seven wishes

On the day of
the feast, crowds came
to cheer and watch
the guests arrive.

The men wore cloaks of the finest velvet and the women shimmered in silks.

Seven fairies flew in
through a castle window,
leaving a glittering trail
behind them.

"The godmothers!" cried
the king, holding out his hands
to greet them.

12

"Let the feast begin!"
announced the queen and
merry music filled the room.

The tables were piled high
with scrumptious food and
everyone ate off golden plates.

When no one could manage
another bite, the fairies
gathered before the king
and queen.

"We have some wishes for
Princess Rose," said Snowdrop,
the first fairy, with a curtsy.

14

She fluttered her fairy fingers.

Rose will be the most beautiful girl in the kingdom...

Then Honeysuckle waved her wand.

...and she'll be clever enough to beat the king at chess!

The third fairy, Willow,
floated over.

She will have grace in all she does.

And she'll dance to perfection,

added Bluebell.

16

Blossom and Buttercup
wished that Rose would...

...play every instrument
like an angel!

and...

...sing like a nightingale.

Everyone wondered what
Jasmine, the seventh and
wisest fairy, would wish for.

17

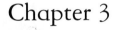

Chapter 3

The uninvited guest

As Jasmine hovered over the cradle, a blast of icy air swept through the Great Hall.

Then a chilling voice
rang out of nowhere. "Haven't
you forgotten someone?"

Suddenly, the mean fairy
Nightshade appeared in a
whirlwind of foul green smoke.

19

"How DARE you not invite me?" she roared.

"W-we didn't mean to, Nightshade," the king stammered. "We just..."

"...forgot you," finished the queen meekly.

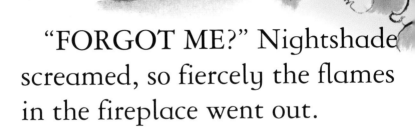

"FORGOT ME?" Nightshade screamed, so fiercely the flames in the fireplace went out.

"Well, you won't forget *this!*" She flicked her cloak and marched up to the cradle.

"Now, my pretty," she purred, lifting a golden curl with a bony finger, "what shall I wish for you?"

Everyone in the palace held their breath. Silent tears ran down the queen's face.

Nightshade leaned into the cradle and snarled, "On your sixteenth birthday, you will prick your finger on a spinning wheel and... DIE!"

"No!" cried the queen. But Nightshade cackled gleefully and disappeared with a deafening bang.

"I still have my wish," said Jasmine softly. "I can't undo that wicked spell, but I can try to change it."

"You *will* prick your finger, little Rose," Jasmine began, "but you won't die. You and everyone else in the castle will fall into a deep sleep."

Only a kiss from your true love will break the spell.

"Burn every spinning wheel in the land at once!" bellowed the king. "Rose must never ever see one!"

That night, the flames from a massive bonfire could be seen for miles. They licked the dark sky like serpents' tongues.

Chapter 4

A special birthday

The years passed and Rose
grew into a delightful girl.
Everyone she met adored her.

She danced, sang
and played music
as wonderfully
as the fairies
had wished.

Ha ha!
Checkmate!

She was clever
and played to win.

Rose loved playing hide-and-seek in the castle gardens.

And, secretly, she liked to sketch the prince of her dreams.

28

Time went happily by and Rose's sixteenth birthday drew near. The castle began to buzz with excitement.

The king and queen were planning a huge ball. Rose was so excited, she could hardly keep still.

Chapter 5

The long sleep

The night of the ball finally
arrived. Handsome princes
and pretty princesses flooded
into the Great Hall.

The king and queen smiled
proudly as they watched Rose
from their thrones.

She swirled and twirled in a
dazzling ball gown and every
prince fell in love with her.

When the feasting was nearly over, Rose pleaded for a game. "Hide-and-seek!" she shouted and dashed off into the castle.

She raced up twisting stairs...

down a
long,
narrow
corridor...

through a tiny door...

...and found herself
at the staircase of
a tower she had
never seen before.

Soft singing floated down
the turret stairs. In a trance,
Rose followed the music.

At the top of the stairs, she
found a heavy iron door.

Inside, an old woman sat
hunched over a spinning wheel.
"Come and see, my pretty,"
she said, beckoning Rose with
a bony finger.

"I'm spinning, my dear," croaked the old woman.

"It's amazing," said Rose, touching the silky thread. "May I try?"

"Of course," said the old woman, taking her hand.

At once, Rose snapped out
of the trance.

"Ow!" she cried,
as she pricked
her finger.

Rose fell to the floor. The
old woman cackled, then
disappeared in a whirlwind
of foul green smoke.

In the same instant, everyone in the castle fell asleep.

The king nodded off over his pudding...

...and the court jester froze mid-leap.

All the clocks stopped.
The place was silent and still...
except for the rose bushes.
They spread like ivy,
covering everything
in their path.

They grew so quickly
that, soon, the entire castle
was covered in thick roots
and sharp thorns.

Chapter 6

A prince rides by

For one hundred years the castle stayed hidden. Only the tops of the towers showed through the bushes. Passers-by stopped to stare at the forgotten castle.

Princes from far and wide heard about the spell. They came in their hundreds to try to rescue the princess known as Sleeping Beauty.

But the thorns cut their skin and the roots wrapped around their legs like snakes. One by one, they gave up.

One day, a brave prince named Florien rode by. He had dreamed of Sleeping Beauty and was determined to find her.

He pulled out his sword with a flourish and began to tackle the spiky bushes.

As Florien's sword touched a
branch, something magical
happened. Each sharp thorn
became a sweet-smelling rose.

A path cleared before him.
He followed its twists and
turns until he reached the
topmost turret and climbed to
where Sleeping Beauty lay.

Florien's heart fluttered like a bird when he saw her. She was the most beautiful girl he had ever seen.

Taking her hand, he kissed her soft lips. Her eyes flickered open and Rose found herself face to face with the prince of her dreams.

"You're the prince I drew!" she cried.

He bowed. "Prince Florien here to rescue you," he announced and scooped her up.

As they walked through tunnels of roses, everyone else in the castle woke up too.

The king fell into his
pudding with a splosh...

...and the court jester landed
with an unexpected bump.

Rose and Florien entered the Great Hall.

"My Rose!" cried the queen.

"And her true love," smiled the king.

Rose and Florien were married the very next day. They lived happily ever after – and the prince always lost at chess.

Sleeping Beauty was first recorded by the French storyteller, Charles Perrault, in 1697, but there have been many different versions since. This version is based on the retelling by Jacob and Wilhelm Grimm, brothers who lived in Germany in the early 1800s.

Series editor: Lesley Sims
Designed by Katarina Dragoslavic

First published in 2006 by Usborne Publishing Ltd., Usborne House, 83-85 Saffron Hill, London EC1N 8RT, England. www.usborne.com
Copyright © 2006 Usborne Publishing Ltd.

48